RUGRATS in Paris THE MOVIE storybook

by Kiki Thorpe
illustrated by Sergio Cuan

Simon Spotlight/Nickelodeon

New York   London   Toronto   Sydney   Singapore

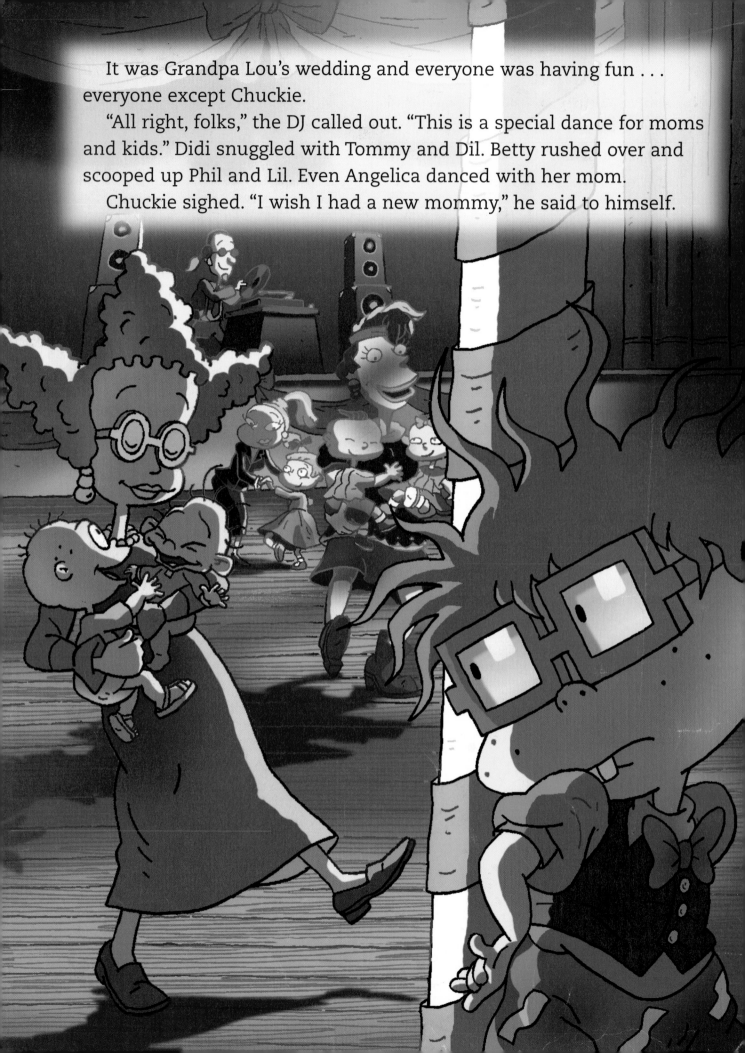

It was Grandpa Lou's wedding and everyone was having fun . . . everyone except Chuckie.

"All right, folks," the DJ called out. "This is a special dance for moms and kids." Didi snuggled with Tommy and Dil. Betty rushed over and scooped up Phil and Lil. Even Angelica danced with her mom.

Chuckie sighed. "I wish I had a new mommy," he said to himself.

Chas thought that Chuckie needed a new mommy too. "I think it's time I start dating again," he told Stu.

Chuckie heard them talking. "What are dates?" he asked the babies.

"Big raisins that make you poop," Phil told him.

Chas went on a lot of dates, but he didn't meet anyone who would be a good mommy for Chuckie.

"This whole thing is giving me a tummy ache," said Chuckie. "I don't think I'm ever gonna find a good mommy."

Late one night the phone rang at the Pickleses' house. Stu picked it up.

"Hello, Mr. Pickles?" a voice said. "I'm calling from Reptarland. The Reptar you designed has broken down. My boss is having a fit."

"Reptar's a hit? That's great," Stu said sleepily.

"We need you to come to Paris on the next flight."

"Ah, the City of Light," Stu murmured.

"Madame recommends—"

"Come with my family and friends?" asked Stu. He yawned. "Okeydokey."

Everyone went to Paris with Stu—even Spike!

Stu decided to take the babies, Angelica, and Chas with him to meet Coco LaBouche, the head of Reptarland. Coco wasn't very happy to see them.

"Call the dogcatcher, the exterminator, do something!" she shouted when she saw Tommy, Chuckie, and the twins crawl into her office.

Fortunately Coco's assistant Kira was nearby. She rescued the babies just in time. "Why don't we take them to the Princess Parade?" Kira suggested to Chas.

"Wow! Isn't this neat, Chuckie?" Tommy exclaimed, watching the samurai warriors wave their swords.

"Look! The princess is coming!" Kira said.

Kira told the babies the story of the Reptar princess: "Once upon a time, there was a mighty dinosaur named Reptar. Everyone ran away from him except the beautiful princess. She was not afraid, for she saw he was lonely and unhappy. With a sprinkling of magic dust, she promised to keep him safe and loved forever and ever."

"Forever and ever," Chuckie repeated as some magic dust landed on his head. He wished the princess would take care of *him* forever and ever.

Back at the office, Coco was talking on the videophone to the president of Reptarland. He was looking for someone to give his job to. "It must be someone who understands what it means to bring joy to children," he told Coco.

Coco hated children, but she wanted to be president. "My childlike heart is bursting with joy," she lied. "I'm about to marry a wonderful man who already has a child."

"I look forward to seeing you with your new family," Mr. Yamaguchi said. "We'll talk about the job then. Good-bye."

"Now where am I going to find a spineless little man with a brat of his own?" she said after Mr. Yamaguchi hung up.

No one noticed that Angelica was hiding under Coco's desk.
Suddenly—*Crash!*—Angelica dropped the bowl of candy she had been
eating. Coco pulled her out from under the desk. "You have five seconds
to come up with a reason why I shouldn't lock you up," she yelled at
Angelica.

"Because I know where you can find a spiny little man with a brat of
his own," Angelica said quickly. She told Coco about Chas and Chuckie.
Suddenly Coco got an idea—she would get Chas to marry her!

The next day Coco invited Chas and the babies to Reptarland. They brought Kira's daughter, Kimi, along too.

"Do you know the princess?" Chuckie asked Kimi.

"No, but I know where she lives," Kimi told him. "Up there in that castle on the bowlcano."

When Coco and Chas weren't looking, the babies climbed on the Ooey-gooey Ride to find the princess.

Kimi led the babies all over Reptarland. "I told you I knew a shortcup," she said when they finally reached the volcano.

"Look, Chuckie! There's the princess!" Tommy cried.

Chuckie could see the princess waving at him. This was his chance to meet her! "Come on, guys!" he shouted.

Meanwhile Coco had discovered that the babies were gone. She ordered the ninja security guards to find them and bring them back.

Chuckie ran toward the castle, but just as he reached the doors, they closed shut. "Oh, no!" he cried.

"Don't worry, Chuckie," Tommy said. "The princess is right inside."

Before Chuckie could do anything, the doorknob turned into a dragon! At least, that's how it looked to Chuckie.

"Nice doggie," Chuckie said, as the dragon began to growl.

Just then a ninja appeared. He grabbed Chuckie and took him back to Coco and Chas.

Chuckie was sad that he didn't get to meet the princess. If only he hadn't been scared! "Next time I see the princess, I'm going to be brave," he promised himself.

That night Chuckie dreamed that he was a fearless karate fighter. Ninjas came at him from every direction, but he fought them all off. In his dream, Chuckie flipped the bad guy over his shoulder and kicked open the door to the princess's castle. Nothing could stop Chuckie!

The next day everyone went to the Princess Spectacular. Chuckie was so excited to see the princess, he didn't even notice Coco sitting next to him. But Angelica did.

"The Finster kid wants a princess for a mom," she told Coco. "And let's face it, lady, you're no princess. See ya!" Angelica ran off before Coco could get mad at her.

But Coco wasn't paying attention to Angelica. She was getting another idea. If Chuckie wanted a princess for a mom, then that's what he would get.

The lights went down. "Welcome to the Princess Spectacular!" the announcer's voice boomed. Chuckie held his breath—maybe now he would finally meet the princess!

A giant Reptar stormed across the stage. Then the princess appeared, singing and dancing. The princess didn't dance very well, and she even knocked Reptar's eye out! But Chuckie didn't notice. He thought she was wonderful.

When the song ended, Chuckie jumped out of his seat and held his Wawa out to the princess. The princess lifted Chuckie into her arms. He had never been happier. But when the princess lowered her fan, Chuckie saw that it was . . .

"Madame LaBouche?!" Kira gasped.

"That mean lady's the princess?" asked Lil.

"She can't be!" Tommy said.

Chuckie was surprised too. But he was even more surprised when he
heard Chas say, "I think Chuckie and I are both in love."

"Well, guys, this is the day I've been waiting for," Chuckie said to his friends. Chas and Coco were getting married; Chuckie was finally going to have a new mom. "It sure is gonna be great having a princess for a mom," he told them. "So how come I don't feel so good?" he added quietly to himself.

Suddenly Coco burst into the room. "What are you doing with that mangy thing?" she yelled, pointing to Chuckie's Wawa. She yanked Chuckie's bear out of his hands.

"Jean-Claude, take these dust mops away!" Coco said angrily. Coco's assistant Jean-Claude locked the babies in a room with the giant Reptar while Coco went off to the wedding.

"Gosh, the princess is really mean," Tommy said.

"She's not anything like I thought she'd be," Chuckie agreed. He started to cry. "My daddy's marrying a lady who doesn't like me or my Wawa or my friends. And it's all my fault."

"Actually, it's sort of my fault," Angelica said. And then she told the babies why Coco wanted to marry Chas.

"What are we going to do?" asked Tommy.

"It's like you always say, Tommy," Chuckie cried, jumping to his feet. "A baby's gotta do what a baby's gotta do. And we gotta stop that wedding!"

When Jean-Claude wasn't looking, the babies climbed into the giant Reptar. Chuckie made the Reptar walk toward the church.

"Way to go, Chuckie!" his friends cheered.

But wait! What was that behind them? Jean-Claude was chasing them in Robosnail!

This time Chuckie wasn't scared. Punching and kicking, Chuckie fought Robosnail. He was a karate superhero, just like in his dream! Chuckie swung hard, and Reptar knocked Robosnail into a river.

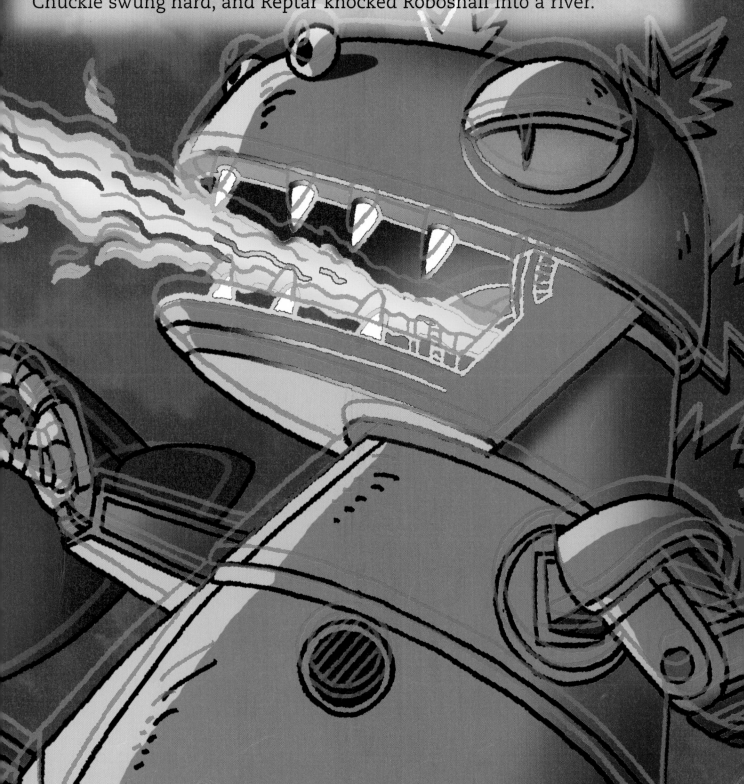

At last the babies reached the church. Chuckie opened the doors and saw Chas and Coco about to be married!

"NOOOOOOOOOOOOOOOOOOOOOOOOOOOOOOO!" he cried.

All the people in the church turned to look at Chuckie.
"Chas, get rid of this little brat!" Coco shouted. Everyone gasped.
"Coco, the wedding is off! You are not the woman for us," Chas told her.
"And you are no longer welcome at Reptarland," said Mr. Yamaguchi.